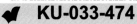

GIRL WONDER AND THE TERRIFIC TWINS

Malorie Blackman is an ex computer-programmer who now writes full time. She has had a number of jobs including database manager, systems programmer, receptionist and shop assistant. As a database manager she travelled extensively to places such as Toronto, Geneva, New York and Dallas.

Not So Stupid! her first collection of short stories was a Selected Twenty title for Feminist Book Fortnight, 1991. Since then she has published over fifteen books, including *Hacker* which won the W H Smith's Mind Boggling Book Award 1994, and the Young Telegraph/Gimme 5 Children's Book of the Year Award 1994, and the *Girl Wonder* series. She has contributed to numerous anthologies for both adults and children. She lives in London with her partner and several pets, including a frog, some bears, an owl, a haggis, a whale and a penguin – all stuffed toys!

Malorie Blackman

GIRL WONDER
and the
Terrific Twins

Illustrated by Lis Toft

PUFFIN BOOKS

PUFFIN BOOKS

Published by the Penguin Group
Penguin Books Ltd, 27 Wrights Lane, London W8 5TZ, England
Penguin Books USA Inc., 375 Hudson Street, New York, New York 10014, USA
Penguin Books Australia Ltd, Ringwood, Victoria, Australia
Penguin Books Canada Ltd, 10 Alcorn Avenue, Toronto, Ontario, Canada M4V 3B2
Penguin Books (NZ) Ltd, 182–190 Wairau Road, Auckland 10, New Zealand

Penguin Books Ltd, Registered Offices: Harmondsworth, Middlesex, England

First published by Victor Gollancz Ltd 1991
Published in Puffin Books 1993
3 5 7 9 10 8 6 4

Typeset by DatIX International Limited, Bungay, Suffolk
Filmset in 14/17pt Monophoto Photina
Printed in Great Britain by Clays Ltd, St Ives plc

To Neil
with love and affection
M.B.

Contents

The Mission
To Rescue
The Football

"Mum, can we play Catch in the garden?" I asked.

"Please, please," said my brother Antony.

"Please, *please*," said my other brother Edward.

Mum's head appeared from beneath the bonnet of her car. She wiped her oily hands on her overalls.

"All right then," Mum said. "But mind the fence by the tree, it's a bit loose. And for goodness sake, keep the ball away from Miss Ree's flowers."

Miss Ree is our moany, old next-door neighbour. She has flowers growing all around her smooth-as-paper lawn. She moans if we even breathe near her flowers. We call her Misery. Miss Ree . . . Mis-ery – get it?

The twins and I ran through the house,

9

grabbed the ball and ran out into the back garden.

It was hot, hot, hot with not a single cloud in the blue sky. We played Piggy-In-The-Middle and Catch for a while.

"I'm hot," complained Antony.

"I'm bored," complained Edward.

"Let's play football instead," I suggested. "We'll each be a team and you only score a goal if you hit the trunk of the apple tree."

"Yeah! Football!" said Antony, clapping his hands.

"Yippee! Football," said Edward, jumping up and down.

We all like football.

I scored the first two goals, then Edward tripped me up and Antony got the ball.

"Cheats! Cheats!" I shouted, chasing after them.

Antony kicked the ball as hard as he could.

"Yah! You missed," I shouted.

Antony didn't miss the tree trunk by inches. He missed it by miles. The ball sailed over the fence into Miss Ree's garden and landed with a SPLOP! Right in her flowerbed.

Antony, Edward and I ran to the fence and looked over.

Oh dear!

If we asked for our ball back, Miss Ree would complain to Mum and then we'd get told off.

So I said, "This is a job for Girl Wonder and . . ."

"The Terrific Twins – hooray!" the twins shouted.

We all spun around until we were getting giddy.

"OK, Terrific Twins, I've got a plan," I said. "We'll climb over the fence and I'll get the ball whilst you two watch for Misery. Make sure you warn me if she's coming."

"OK, Girl Wonder," said Antony.

So we all started to clamber over the fence.

CRR . . . RR . . . EAK!

CRR . . . RR . . . UNCH!

The whole fence fell flat – right on to Miss

Ree's flowerbed. And with us on top of it! We were sprawled out and wondering what had happened. Miss Ree's kitchen door burst open. Then our kitchen door was flung open.

"My roses! My lupins! My begonias!" Miss Ree wailed.

"My goodness!" Mum said, running out of the kitchen.

"Just look what they've done to my flowers," Miss Ree said to Mum. Mum put her hands on her hips. Her face was like dark grey clouds just before thunder and lightning.

"Maxine, Antony, Edward, what have you been doing now?" Mum said.

"We just wanted to get our ball, Mum," I said as we all stood up.

"I'm sorry about your flowers, Miss Ree," Mum said. "Don't worry. I'll fix the fence and we'll replace all the flowers."

Then Mum called us into the house.

She told us off in the kitchen. She told us off in the car as we drove to the garden centre. She told us off as we picked out new flowers and rose bushes. She told us off as we drove back home. She told us off as she fixed the fence. She told us off as we all pulled the scrushed, crushed flowers out of the ground and planted the new ones.

Whilst Mum was resting her mouth for a second, I whispered to Antony, "There's our ball. Run and get it and throw it back into our garden."

Before Mum could say anything, Antony did just that.

Once we had replanted Miss Ree's new flowers and rose bushes, Mum called us into the house again.

"Can we take our ball and go to the park?" I asked.

"No you cannot. You three can stay *in* for

the rest of the day and stay *out* of trouble,"
Mum said.

So after we'd washed our hands and faces
and changed our clothes, the twins and I sat
on the carpet in the living-room playing Snap.

"Your plan was stupid," Antony grumbled.

"Yeah! Silly-stupid," said Edward.

"But it worked, didn't it?" I said. "We *did*
get our ball back!"

Staying Cool
At The
Swimming Pool

It was bright, burning hot.

So hot the branches on our apple tree drooped.

So hot Miss Ree's flowers hung their heads.

So hot I was sure I was going to melt at any second.

"What shall we do today!" I muttered.

"It's too hot to do anything," Antony murmured.

"Yeah! Too hot!" Edward mumbled.

Mum fanned herself with the newspaper. "We all need to do something to cool us down. I know! Let's go swimming."

"Swimming! Yeah!" I said.

"Swimming! Hooray!" Antony shouted.

"Swimming! Yippee!" Edward clapped his hands.

So we got our swimming costumes and

some towels and Mum drove us to the swimming pool. When we'd all changed into our swimming costumes, Mum led us down to the pool.

"I want all three of you to stay near me," Mum said. "And you're not to go anywhere near the deep end."

We reached the pool. It was jam-packed solid full of people. And all around the edge of the pool were mums and dads.

"Oh dear! I should have realized it would be this crowded. Everyone's had the same idea as us," Mum sighed.

We got into the pool at the shallow end. We couldn't even walk from one side of the pool to the other without bumping into someone, let alone swim. But at least we were wet and cool.

"It's so hot . . ."

"I wish I was in there. I'm so uncomfortable . . ."

I looked up at the man and woman who had just spoken. The woman wiped the perspiration off her forehead whilst the man used his hand to fan himself. Everyone around the pool seemed really uncomfortable. They were all looking longingly at the water.

"Look at those people," I whispered to Antony and Edward. "We should do something to cool them down."

"What?" Antony asked.

"Yeah! What?" Edward repeated.

So I said, "I think this is a job for Girl Wonder and . . ."

"The Terrific Twins!" Antony and Edward splashed up and down in the water. Then we spun around as fast as we could in the water – which wasn't fast at all so we soon gave up on that.

"OK, Terrific Twins, I have a plan," I said. "We're going to help cool down all those people around the pool who are watching."

"Why?" Antony asked.

"Yeah! Why?" Edward repeated.

"Because we're super heroes. We must help people," I said.

"How?" Antony asked.

"Yeah! How?" Edward repeated.

"How about if we jog past all those hot, sticky, sweaty people, splattering them with drops of cold water? That would cool them down," I suggested.

"Good idea," said Antony.

"Yeah! Good idea!" said Edward.

"Where are you lot going?" Mum asked as we got out of the pool.

"Just for a walk, Mum," I said.

"Well, be careful and stay away from the deep end," Mum replied.

We walked to the opposite corner of the pool.

"Ready, Terrific Twins?" I asked.

"Ready!"

The three of us formed a line and jogged along shaking our hands and heads as we went and splattering the grown-ups with water. I must admit, they didn't look too pleased.

Then Antony bumped into one woman who was thin like string. Her arms spun around as she tried to keep her balance. She grabbed the man wearing glasses next to her who grabbed the bald man next to him. The thin woman yelled as she plunged into the pool followed by the man with glasses, then the bald man. As the bald man was falling he grabbed the arm of the woman next to him. Everyone was grabbing everyone else to stop themselves from falling into the pool – but it didn't help. The whole line of men and women tumbled into the water.

SPLOSH! SPLASH!

"Oh dear!" I muttered.

Mum came running up to us.

"Maxine, Antony, Edward, what have you three rascals been doing now?" Mum asked. "And you should have more sense than to run around a swimming pool. It's dangerous. You might have slipped."

I looked in the pool at all those men and women, coughing and spluttering and wringing out their shirts and jackets and dresses. They were all glaring at us. It looked like we were the only ones who *hadn't* slipped.

"What were you three doing?" Mum asked, her hands on her hips. But we didn't get the chance to explain. We got chucked out of the swimming pool. Mum was *so* embarrassed.

All the way home all she kept saying was, "I'll never live this down . . . I'll never live this down."

"Your plan was feeble," Antony mumbled in the back seat next to me.

"Yeah! Foolish-feeble," Edward grumbled.

"But it worked, didn't it?" I said. "We did cool down all those people."

Rescuing The Rescuers

"I want a dog," I said.

"I want a cat," said Antony.

"I want a rabbit," said Edward.

Mum put her hands on her hips. "I'm not getting three different pets. In fact I'm not sure I should even get one."

"But . . ." I said.

"But . . ." said Antony.

"But . . ." Edward repeated.

"No buts!" Mum argued. "I don't think you three realize how much work is involved in owning a pet."

"We do!" I said.

"We do!" said Antony.

"We do!" Edward repeated.

Then Mum got a funny look in her eyes. The same look she gets when she has one of her ideas and she thinks it's a good one.

I wonder why her ideas always seem to get me and the twins into trouble?

"Stay there you three. I'll be right back," Mum said, and off she dashed.

My brothers and I looked at each other and shrugged. Before we got bored just standing and waiting, Mum came back with a large box in her hands.

"What's in the box?" we asked.

Mum put the box down on the carpet. We peered into it.

"A cat!" I said, surprised.

"It's Mr McBain's cat. Her name is Syrup because she's the exact same colour as golden syrup."

Mr McBain is our other next-door neighbour. He's a tall, elderly man with hair that only grows on the sides of his head. The top of his head is shiny and smooth like an egg.

"How come we've got her?" Antony asked.

"Yeah! How come?" asked Edward.

"If you three can look after Syrup for this weekend without getting into trouble then we'll talk seriously about which pet to get – but only then," Mum said.

"What do we do first?" I asked.

Antony, Edward and I knelt down around the box.

"First, take Syrup out of the box. Then take her litter tray out of the box and put it in the conservatory near the washing machine. Then you can feed her. Mr McBain also gave me two tins of cat food. They're in my trouser pockets. After that you can play with her," Mum said.

So I picked Syrup out of the box and held her against my chest and stroked her. She was warm and her fur was soft. Her breath tickled my face. I liked her.

"Maybe we should have a cat and not a dog," I thought.

Antony took out Syrup's litter tray and put it in the conservatory. Edward got the two tins of cat food out of Mum's tracksuit trouser pockets.

"Later on we'll all have to pop to the shop at the top of the road and get some more cat food," said Mum.

Mum opened one of the tins and put the food in Syrup's bowl which was also in the box. We all crouched down around Syrup as she ate.

"I want a cat, Mum," I said.

"So do I," Antony said.

"Yeah! Me too!" said Edward.

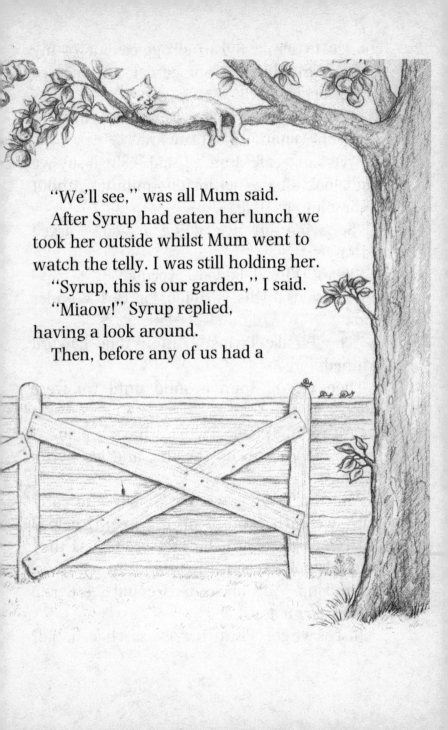

"We'll see," was all Mum said.

After Syrup had eaten her lunch we took her outside whilst Mum went to watch the telly. I was still holding her.

"Syrup, this is our garden," I said.

"Miaow!" Syrup replied, having a look around.

Then, before any of us had a

chance to blink, Syrup struggled out of my arms, scurried across our garden and scooted up our apple tree.

"What do we do now?" Antony asked.

"Yeah! What?" asked Edward.

"We can't call Mum," I said. "She'll say we can't look after a pet for one minute without getting into trouble."

"So what *are* we going to do?" asked Antony.

"Yeah! What?" Edward repeated.

So I said, "This is a job for Girl Wonder and . . ."

"The Terrific Twins!" Antony and Edward grinned.

Then we all spun around until we were dizzy.

"All right, Terrific Twins, I have a plan," I said. "We'll climb up the tree and get Syrup down."

And that's what we did. Slowly and carefully, we each climbed up the tree. (I helped the twins get on to the first branch as they couldn't quite reach it.) Up and up we went. Up and up. And above us I could see Syrup staring down at us.

Just as we got close to her, guess what she did?

She yawned. She stretched her back. Then she scooted *down* the tree.

"Huh! Why didn't she do that *before* we came up here?" I said.

We all looked down. The ground looked far, *far* away.

"What are you kids up to?" Mr McBain called out from his garden.

"What do you children think you're doing?" shouted Miss Ree from her garden. "Get down at once before you hurt yourselves."

I looked at Antony and Edward and they looked at me. Then we all burst into tears.

"We can't get down," I sobbed. "The ground is far, *far* away."

Then Mum came running out into the garden.

"Maxine, Antony, Edward, what have you been doing now?" she said, her hands on her hips.

"We were trying to rescue the cat," I sniffed.

"Maxine, cats climb up trees all the time. Unlike you lot, they have no trouble climbing down either. You should have left Syrup up there," Mr McBain said.

"Mum, I want to come down," wailed Antony.

"Yeah! Me too!" Edward joined in.

"I'm going to have to call the Fire Brigade," Mum said.

Within minutes we heard the sound of the fire engine siren – DRING DRING DRING DRING! Mum ran into the house to let them in. Seconds later she came out into the garden followed by a firewoman and three firemen. They all stood below our apple tree. We peered down at them. We'd never seen firepeople up close before. The firemen placed two ladders against the trunk of the tree.

"It's all right. We'll soon have you down," said the firewoman.

"Don't worry," said one of the firemen. "You'll soon be on the ground."

They carried Antony and Edward down first. I looked around. I could see across all the neighbours' gardens. *Everyone* was watching us.

"All right, Maxine, take my hands," said the firewoman, lifting me round on to her back. "I'm going to give you a piggyback ride. In Scotland we call it a collybucky."

"A collybucky! That's a funny name." I laughed.

"No funnier than piggyback," said the firewoman. "Here we are down on the ground."

I looked around, surprised. I hadn't even noticed us coming down.

"Say thank you to the firepeople," Mum said.

"Thank you very much," we said.

"Right, you three – go into the house. I've got a few things to say to you," Mum said sternly. "And Syrup is going straight back to Mr McBain."

We went into the kitchen and looked through the window. Mum was talking to the firepeople.

"Mum's going to spend for ever telling us off now," Antony said to me, annoyed.

"Yeah! For ever!" Edward agreed.

"Your plan was stinky," Antony grumbled.

"Yeah! Seriously stinky," Edward mumbled.

"But it worked, didn't it?" I said. "We *did* get Syrup out of the tree."

Captain,
The Teddy-Bear Dog

The next day we decided to try again. WE WANTED A PET!

"Mum..." Antony said slowly. "We're sorry about what happened yesterday."

"Yeah, we're sorry," Edward said.

"Very sorry," I added.

"Hhmm!" was all Mum said.

"Can we have another chance, please?" Antony asked. "I'd do anything to get a cat..."

"A rabbit..." said Edward.

"A..."

"A nothing," Mum interrupted, her hands on her hips. "I have no intention of getting a pet for you three. Not after I had to call out the Fire Brigade yesterday. You had that cat for just five minutes and you still managed to get into trouble."

"Oh, please . . ." we all begged.

"NO! And that's final." And Mum turned back to picking the bad rice grains out of the rice.

My brothers and I wandered out into the garden. We sat on the grass and I started to pull the grass blades out of the ground.

"It's all your fault, Maxine," Antony said, pouting at me. "It was your idea to go up the tree after Syrup the cat."

"Yeah, your fault," Edward agreed.

"No it wasn't."

"Yes it was."

"No it wasn't."

"Yes it was."

Then we had a big argument about whose fault it was until Mum tapped on the kitchen window and made a stern face which said, "I hope you three aren't arguing" without the words even having to come out of her mouth.

"The thing is, what are we going to do now?" I said. "We've got to persuade Mum to buy us a pet."

"That's a hard one," said Antony.

"Yeah! Hard!" agreed Edward.

"I think this is definitely a job for Girl Wonder . . ."

"And the Terrific Twins," said Antony and Edward glumly.

This was definitely a tough one! We sat and thought and thought.

"Terrific Twins, I've got it!" I said at last, clapping my hands together. "We'll prove to Mum that we can look after a pet."

"She'll never allow us to have Syrup back," Antony said. "So how are we going to look after a pet without actually having a pet to practise on?"

"Yeah! How?" asked Edward.

"We'll use Captain, my teddy bear, and pretend it's a dog . . ."

"A cat . . ." said Antony.

"A rabbit," said Edward.

"Do you two want to hear my plan or not?" I asked, folding my arms across my chest.

"Get on with it then," Antony said.

"Yeah, hurry up," Edward added.

Brothers!

"As I was saying, we'll have to pretend Captain is our pet and show Mum that we can look after him. And Captain will be a dog because he's my teddy bear and it was my idea."

So we all agreed and went indoors to start our plan. I ran up to my bedroom and brought Captain downstairs. I put him in front of the telly. Then the twins and I sat on the sofa.

"You three are very quiet. What are you doing?" Mum asked as she walked into the room. Then she saw Captain. "Maxine, why have you brought your teddy bear downstairs?"

"Captain isn't a teddy bear. Captain is our pet dog," Antony said.

A slow smile spread over Mum's face. "Oh, is he?" she said. "So you'll be taking him for a walk before lunch."

"That's right," I replied, peeved because Mum was biting her bottom lip. She always does that when she's trying not to laugh, and this was serious!

Mum went out into the kitchen and came back with a piece of string with a loop at one end. "There you are, a lead for your dog," she said, biting her lip after each word.

I put the lead around Captain's neck.

"Come on you two, we've got to take Captain for a walk," I said.

"I'm not walking down the street dragging a teddy bear." Antony frowned.

"Nor am I," said Edward.

"I thought it was a dog!" Mum laughed.

"It's a dog in the house," Antony said. "Outside the house it's a teddy bear."

Antony and Edward refused to take Captain for a walk with me. So that was the end of that idea. When Mum left the room I said, "All right then. We'll have to come up with another plan to persuade Mum to buy us a pet."

"Like what?" Antony asked.

"Such as?" asked Edward.

Get A Pet –
Plan Two

"If we want a pet, we're going to have to come up with a super-duper-mega-ace plan," I replied. "So this is a job that only Girl Wonder . . ."

"And the Terrific Twins can do," Edward finished, and we all spun around until the room spun with us.

We sat very still and thought very hard.

"How about . . ." I began slowly. "How about if we're very good and help Mum around the house and then she'll forget about yesterday?"

"Hhmm!" said Antony.

"Hhhmmm!" Edward repeated.

"It's worth a try, unless either of you has a better idea."

They didn't. We walked into the kitchen.

"Do you want some help, Mum?" we asked as she started the washing-up.

"Some help doing what?" Mum asked suspiciously.

"Some help with the washing-up," I answered.

Mum looked really suspicious now. "There's only three saucepans and a couple of plates, but all right then. Edward and Antony, you can wash up, and Maxine you can dry."

"All right, Mum," we said.

Mum put her hands on her hips. "What are you three up to now?"

"Nothing. We're just helping you – that's all."

"Hhmm!" Mum replied. "All right then, but no messing about with the hot water or you'll scald yourselves."

Antony put on Mum's rubber gloves as Mum left the kitchen, shaking her head.

"Don't drop any plates," I hissed at the twins.

Antony ran some cold water into the sink, then a little bit of hot water. Then he squeezed some washing-up liquid under the running taps – and he squeezed and he SQUEEZED. The bump of bubbles in the sink grew into a hill of bubbles and the hill turned into a mountain of bubbles. We stared at the *world* of bubbles which was still growing.

"How much washing-up liquid did you squeeze into the sink?" I asked Antony.

"All of it." Antony frowned. "Wasn't I supposed to?"

"I don't think so," I replied. "Quick, do something."

Edward swept his hand through the bubbles. They flew everywhere – over the draining board, over the plants on the window-sill. They floated up towards the ceiling and they floated down towards the floor.

"Maxine, do something," Antony said quickly.

Then the water in the sink began to splosh over on to the kitchen floor.

"Turn off the taps. Quick!" I said.

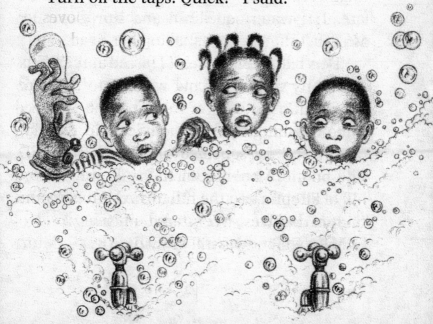

Antony turned off the taps but it was too late. The water squelched and slurped under our feet.

"That's the end of my cat . . ." Antony sighed.

"That's the end of my rabbit . . ." Edward shrugged.

"Get some kitchen towels," I said quickly. "Don't let Mum see this . . ."

"Don't let Mum see what?"

We all spun around. There was Mum in the kitchen doorway, her hands on her hips.

'MAXINE! ANTONY! EDWARD!" Mum

42

roared. "What is that?" She pointed to the mega-enormous universe of bubbles behind us. "And what's that?" She pointed to the water puddle under our feet.

"It's . . . er . . ."

"Never mind. Antony, pull out the plug from the sink," Mum ordered. Then she stood over us as we mopped up the floor and wiped down the sink and wiped each leaf on every plant – which took *mega-ages*. And of all the telling-offs Mum had ever given us, the one we got as we cleaned up the kitchen was the best! (By that I mean the longest and the most cross!) We tried to tell Mum that we'd only been trying to help but she wouldn't listen.

"Trying to help!" she fumed. "Trying to help! A hurricane would have been more helpful."

"Does that mean you won't buy us a pet?" Antony asked. I could have kicked him.

"So that's what this is all about," Mum retorted. "Right, that does it. Tomorrow I'm going to get you a pet and that'll be the end of that."

"Get a cat. Please, *please*," pleaded Antony.

"No, don't. Get a rabbit. Please, Mum," begged Edward.

"A dog would be the most interesting, Mum . . ." I began.

Mum raised her hand. "That's enough – from all three of you. I have already made up my mind which pet we're going to have."

We tried to ask Mum which pet she was going to get but all she did was raise her arm even higher.

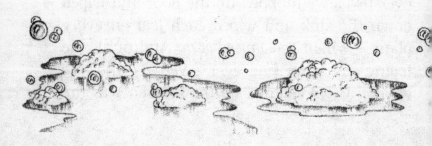

"Ask me no questions and I'll tell you no lies," she said. "Now off you go into the garden."

And Mum didn't mention our pet for the rest of the day.

The next morning we peered out of the window, waiting for Mum to return from the pet shop. At last she came walking up the garden path, a small brown bag in her hand.

"That's much too tichy for a kitten." Antony frowned.

"That bag is too tiny for a rabbit," said Edward.

"That bag is too tiddly for a puppy," I said.

We ran out to meet Mum.

"What is it? What is it?" we asked eagerly.

Mum pulled off the brown bag. In her hand she held a small polythene bag filled with water and in the water was a tiny goldfish.

"This is your pet," Mum said.

A goldfish!

"The tank is in the car next to the fish food

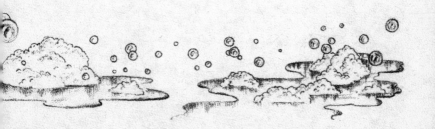

on the passenger seat. Maxine, you get the tank and carry it *carefully*. Boys, you can get the fish food."

"A goldfish!" Antony said when we got to the car. "That's not much of a pet. It can't catch mice like a cat."

"Or munch lettuce and carrots like a rabbit," said Edward.

"Or fetch a stick like a dog," I sighed.

"So much for your silly-stupid-seriously-stinky-smelly plan, Maxine," Antony pouted.

"Huh!" I replied. "We got a pet, didn't we? And a goldfish is better than nothing."

As Tall As Tall

I was in a bad mood when I got home from school.

"What's the matter with you?" Antony asked.

"Yeah, what's the matter?" asked Edward.

I stared at myself in the hall mirror. I turned to the left and I turned to the right.

"Do you think I'm short?" I asked my brothers.

"You're taller than us," said Antony.

"A lot taller," agreed Edward.

"But I'm not as tall as Sharon in my class at school. She's taller than everyone – except the teacher."

"So?" said Antony.

"She called me a short dumpling," I frowned. "I need to grow taller – a lot taller. I want to be taller than Sharon. I want to be as tall as tall."

"How are you going to do that?" Antony asked.

"Yeah, how?" asked Edward.

"I'll have to think about that one," I replied.

"Maybe this is a job for Girl Wonder and . . ."

"The Terrific Twins!" my brothers shouted, whirling around like spinning tops.

"We need a plan – something that will make me grow," I said. "Come on Terrific Twins – I need your help. Think!"

We sat down on the carpet, each of us crossing our legs. We each sat very still and thought and thought. I thought so hard that my eyes began to ache.

"How tall do you want to grow?" asked Antony. "Do you want to grow as tall as a mountain or only as tall as a tree?"

I thought for a moment. "As tall as a tree," I decided.

That would be tall enough.

We each thought some more.

"Well, if you plant a little seed it grows into a big tree," Edward said. "So maybe if you swallowed a little seed, it would grow into a big tree inside you and it would push you up and up and then you'd be as tall as a tree. You'd be as tall as tall."

"That's a good idea!" I grinned. "I'll swallow orange seeds. Orange trees are tall and I can get the seeds because we always have plenty of oranges in the house. Are you two going to join me?"

"Nah! We'll watch you first to see if it works," Antony said.

"Yeah, we'll watch you first," Edward agreed.

Just then Mum came in from the garage.

"Right then. What would you three like for your tea?" Mum asked.

"Fish and chips," said Antony.

"Sausages and chips," said Edward, clapping his hands.

"Oranges!" I shouted.

Mum just laughed. I think she thought I was joking.

In the end Mum made fish and chips. I didn't have any even though it smelt scrummy-delicious. I had to leave room for my oranges. Whilst the twins and Mum scoffed the scrummy-delicious fish and chips I chewed on my oranges, swallowing the seeds whole.

"Why are you eating so many oranges?" Mum asked me.

"I like oranges," I replied, trying to force down the last orange.

Mum looked at me, her eyes suspicious. All she said was "Hhmm!"

The next day I had two oranges for breakfast, three oranges for lunch and four oranges for dinner. As soon as dinner was finished I measured myself against our measuring wall in the bathroom. I hadn't grown one millimetre! And what's more I was sick – sick of oranges.

When I woke up the next morning I had the worst tummy ache in the world.

"Ooh!" I groaned. "Ooooh!"

Mum called the doctor.

"Now then, Maxine," Doctor Turner said after taking my temperature, "your mum told me that you're eating a lot of oranges. She said you're eating oranges and nothing else. Is that right?"

I nodded. Oooooooh! My stomach was really hurting.

"Why have you suddenly become so keen on oranges?" Doctor Turner asked.

Mum was glaring at me from beside Doctor Turner. She had her hands on her hips.

"I love oranges." I didn't exactly lie, but I didn't exactly tell the truth either.

"Is that the *whole* reason?" Mum asked softly.

I thought hard. My stomach ache was getting worse and I was as miserable as miserable but I didn't want to tell Mum why I was eating so many oranges. She might stop me, or worse still she might get annoyed.

"Yeah, that's the whole reason," I replied.

"Doctor Turner, can I speak to you for a moment?" Mum said.

The doctor and my mum went outside my room to stand on the landing.

"I . . . oranges . . . cure . . . oranges . . . oranges . . . oranges . . ." That was all I heard, even though I pushed my ears as far forward as possible.

Mum and Doctor Turner came back into the room.

"Maxine, Doctor Turner agrees with me that what you need is a diet of oranges and nothing else," Mum began. "I *was* going to make you a cheese, onion and potato pie, followed by ice-cream and chocolate sauce and a long glass of ice-cold cream soda, but . . ."

"It's all right," I said quickly. "I don't mind having that."

"Nonsense," Mum smiled. "You said you love oranges. That's all you've eaten for the last two days."

"But just to make sure that Maxine gets all her essential vitamins and minerals, I would prescribe two tablespoonfuls of cod-liver oil three times a day and a chewy vitamin tablet twice a day," said Doctor Turner, scribbling on a pad. "That way Maxine can eat as many oranges as she likes and nothing else."

"NO! I DON'T WANT ANY MORE ORANGES," I pleaded. "Maybe . . . maybe I'm not so keen on them after all."

"Then why were you eating so many of them?" Mum asked.

Her eyes were glinting and sparking like when the sun shines on water. When she looks at me like that, it's as if she can read my mind. I decided that perhaps I should just tell the truth. The truth takes a lot less effort.

"Well . . . Sharon at school called me a short dumpling," I muttered. "So I was swallowing orange seeds so that they would grow into a tree inside me and push me up. Then I'd be taller than Sharon and she couldn't call me a short dumpling any more."

"Oh, I see." Doctor Turner laughed.

"Oh, I see." Mum smiled.

"Maxine, it's the oranges that are causing your stomach ache," Doctor Turner said.

"And it doesn't matter how many you eat, you'll never get a tree growing inside of you. If you want to grow you have to eat lots of different kinds of foods – like carrots and greens, and protein foods like eggs and milk."

"Yuk!" I said. "What about chocolate? Will that make me grow?"

"Only sideways, not upwards," smiled Doctor Turner.

"Maxine, you're not short and it wouldn't matter if you were," Mum said. "It's what you are inside that counts, not what you are outside. Do you understand?"

"Yes, Mum," I said, holding my aching stomach.

"OK, Maxine, I'll prescribe some medicine for you which should take away your stomach ache. No more oranges or you'll turn into one," said Doctor Turner, pulling a face.

I smiled up at her. She's funny.

Mum went downstairs, followed by the doctor. After a few minutes Mum came back up the stairs alone, her hands behind her back.

"I've brought you a drink." Mum smiled, her eyes glinting.

"What is it?" I asked suspiciously.

Mum brought out the glass from behind her

back. "Orange juice!" She laughed.

I buried my head under my pillow. "Take it away!" I said. "I never want to see anything that's orange ever again."

Saving Energy

When I got home from school, I ran into the kitchen where Mum was mashing potatoes for our tea and the twins were laying the table.

"What did you do at school today?" Mum asked me.

"We learnt about energy and how we should all save it," I replied, dropping my school bag on the kitchen lino. "We should always switch off lights when we're not in the room and we should switch off all electric appli . . . appli . . . appliances when we're not using them."

"Quite right too," Mum said. "Mind you, I've been telling you and your brothers to save energy for years and you haven't listened to one word yet."

"Oh, we will now," I said.

"Why?" Antony asked.

"Yeah, why?" Edward repeated.

"Because the more energy we save the longer it will last us and the less we waste."

"What sort of waste?" Antony asked.

"Well . . ."

"Maxine means things like not filling a kettle with water when all you want is one cup of tea. It takes more energy and longer to heat up a full kettle than a half full one," Mum said.

"Hhmm!" Edward said.

"Maxine, could you spoon out the mashed potato on to the plates next to the sausages. I'll be right back."

When Mum left the room, I said to the twins, "I think we should make sure that we save energy."

"How?" Edward said, for once getting in before Antony.

"Hhmm!" I thought. "We're going to need a good plan. I think maybe this is a job for Girl Wonder . . ."

"And the Terrific Twins! Yippee!" shouted the twins. And we spun around until we all fell down.

"How about . . . how about if we make sure that everything is switched off before we go to bed tonight?" Antony suggested.

"We could go into each room and make sure that all the lights and things are switched off," Edward continued.

"That sounds like a good idea," I grinned. "All right then, I'll do upstairs and you two can do downstairs."

"How come we get the downstairs?" Antony protested.

"Yeah, how come?" repeated Edward.

"Because downstairs is bigger and there are two of you," I explained.

"Hhmm!" they both said, but they didn't argue so I got away with it.

After our tea of fat sausages and peas and mashed potatoes, we all sat down to watch telly.

"Mum, shouldn't we switch off the telly to save energy?" Edward asked.

Mum laughed. "But we're watching it. We can't save energy by switching it off and watch it at the same time."

"But it *would* save energy if we *did* switch it off, wouldn't it?" Edward persisted.

"Yes it would," Mum agreed. "But I'm not going to. I like this programme."

Edward leaned over and whispered to Antony and me, "Let's not watch it. Let's do something else – then that would save energy."

"I don't think it works like that," I frowned. "The telly uses the same amount of energy whether only Mum watches it or all four of us watch it."

So we watched telly until it was time for us to go to bed.

"I'm a bit tired, so I think I'll have an early night as well," Mum yawned, switching off the telly and pulling out the plug.

We cleaned our teeth and put on our pyjamas. Then, when Mum was in the bathroom, I grabbed my brothers.

"Come on Terrific Twins. Now's our chance to save energy. You two do the kitchen and the conservatory and the living-room and I'll do the bedrooms," I said.

Five minutes later we met back upstairs.

"We've saved energy everywhere," the twins said proudly.

"So have I," I said. "Goodnight Antony, goodnight Edward. See you in the morning."

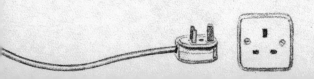

Mum read to the twins first, then she came into my bedroom and read me a fairy story. I love fairy stories.

"Goodnight Maxine." Mum smiled, and she switched off the bedroom light and closed the door behind her. Then I fell asleep, dreaming of the ways I could save energy.

"MAXINE, ANTONY, EDWARD – GET DOWN HERE! THIS MINUTE!"

I rubbed my eyes. It was morning but I was still sleepy.

"MAXINE! EDWARD! ANTONY! NOW!"

I didn't like the sound of Mum's voice. It sounded crosser than cross. I hopped out of bed and walked down the stairs behind the twins.

"What's the matter?" I whispered to them.

"I don't know," Antony whispered back.

"Nor do I," Edward mouthed.

We walked into the kitchen where Mum was. Her hands were folded across her chest and her eyes were glaring at us.

I knew we were in BIG TROUBLE.

"Which one of you ninnies switched off the fridge last night?" Mum asked.

I looked at the twins. They looked at me. No one spoke.

"I'm waiting for an answer," Mum said. "I'll have you know that all the ice in the freezer has melted because one of you three pulled out the plug for the fridge. The ice-cream has melted all over my mince and the fridge is one great big sticky mess. It's full of water and there's water all over the floor."

Still no one said a word.

"And which one of you twits switched off the washing machine when it was in the middle of washing my jumpers?" Mum ranted. "Now all my jumpers have shrunk. They're ruined."

The twins and I looked at each other. We stayed silent.

"And which one of you pea-heads pulled out the plug for the video recorder. I wanted to tape a late night film and I MISSED IT!"

Antony started to sniff, then to sob. "I . . . I pulled out the plug for the fridge. I was only trying to save energy like Maxine said. And I was . . . I was the one who pulled out . . . pulled out the video recorder plug."

Edward started to howl. "I pulled out the plug for the washing machine. I was only trying to save energy like Maxine said we should."

"I never told you to pull out every plug in the house," I protested. "Mum, that's not fair . . ."

"That's enough. Right then," Mum's hands

were on her hips. "All three of you are going to clean up this kitchen until it's spotless. And all three of you will get no more pocket money until you've paid for my ruined jumpers."

And Mum marched out of the kitchen.

We got out the mop and some squeezy-cloths and started mopping up the floor.

"It's all your fault," Antony said.

"Yeah, *all* your fault," Edward agreed. "You

were the one who came home and said we should save energy."

"It was your idea to check and make sure we'd saved energy before we went to bed," I told the twins.

"But it was all your idea in the first place," Antony said.

"I'm not talking to you two," I said in a huff.

"And we're not talking to you either," Antony whinged. "Your idea was mega-super-duper-ginormous-galactic stinky. We didn't save *our* energy. My arms are killing me."

"Mine too," Edward agreed, giving me a dirty look.

Huh! Sometimes being a super heroine is no fun!

Beware The Park Bench

We were going to Aunt Joanne and Uncle Stan's house.

Their house is neat and clean and . . . really boring! They don't have one single book on the floor. They don't have any comics on the chairs. Their kitchen never has dirty forks and spoons lying about in the sink. It's not like our house at all.

We always have to dress up in our best clothes when we visit Uncle Stan and Aunt Joanne. Even Mum dresses up.

As it was a sunny day, Mum decided that we could walk through the park. Our aunt and uncle live just on the other side of the park. So off we went.

"Maxine, Antony, Edward, make sure you keep your clothes spotless," Mum warned. "So there is to be no messing about."

As if we would!

The park was full of people.

"Mum, can I go on the swings? Please, *please?*" I asked.

"No. You'll get your dress dirty," replied Mum.

"Mum, can I go on the roundabout?" Antony asked.

"Yeah! The roundabout," Edward repeated.

"No. You'll get your clothes creased," Mum said.

I didn't see the point of going through the park if you couldn't run and jump and play in the playground.

"Oh, look at that," I said.

Near us, a girl and a boy were flying a kite. It danced in the sky. We all stopped to watch.

"Mum, do you know how to make a kite?" I asked.

"Yes. I'll show you when we get back home. It's really easy," Mum said.

"Hooray!" we all shouted.

That cheered us up.

We were just passing by a park bench when I noticed something very strange. There were two spiders trying to swing down from the

bench but they weren't getting very far. They scurried a little way along the bench and then tried to swing down but they never got all their legs off the bench. Then they scurried further along the bench and tried again but the same thing happened.

"Mum, look at that," I pointed.

"How strange!" Mum said. "They can't get down."

And we all stopped to watch the spiders.

"Antony, Edward, do you know what I think?" I whispered to them.

"No, what?" Antony asked.

"Yeah! What?" Edward repeated.

So I said, "I think this is a job for Girl Wonder and . . ."

"The Terrific Twins!" my brothers whispered back.

And we spun around until the park was spinning with us.

"What on earth are you three doing?" Mum laughed.

"It's a secret," I told Mum.

"Well, come on. We can't stand here all day," Mum said.

"But Mum, can't we help the spiders?" Antony asked.

"Yeah! Can't we do something? They want to get down," Edward said.

"Oh, all right then," Mum replied.

She doesn't like spiders much. We all sat down on the bench and watched the spiders some more. Then I saw a piece of brown cardboard propped up against the side of the park bench.

"I've got a plan," I said to the twins as I leaned over to get it. "This piece of cardboard will help the spiders to get to the ground."

I leaned one end of the piece of cardboard against the bench and the other end I placed against the ground so that the piece of cardboard was like a slide.

"Come on, Mr and Mrs Spider," I said. "We haven't got all day."

"No, we haven't," Mum agreed, glancing down at her watch.

The spiders hopped on to the cardboard immediately and scuttled down on to the ground.

"Come on, then," Mum said, and she went to stand up. Only she had trouble. It was like she was sticking to the bench.

"What on earth . . .?" Mum said.

She put her hand down on the bench. Then she looked at the palm of her hand. It was bright green.

"This bench is wet!" Mum said, springing up off the bench. "Stand up you three."

We stood up.

"Turn around," Mum ordered.

We turned around.

"Oh no!" Mum cried. "Just look at your best clothes!"

We twisted our heads to look at our backs. I

pulled the back of my dress skirt out to look at it. It was covered in green paint.

"Why didn't they leave a warning here to say the bench had just been painted?" Mum asked furiously, her hands on her hips.

She was seriously, *seriously* annoyed!

Then she looked down at the cardboard slide I had used to get the spiders to the ground. She picked it up and turned it over. Then showed it to us. There on the sign, in big green letters, it said:

BEWARE!! WET PAINT!!

"Maxine, where did you get this sign from?" Mum asked.

"From beside the bench," I replied.

"Why didn't you read it before we all sat down and ruined our clothes? That's why the spiders couldn't get down. Their feet kept sticking to the paint," Mum said. "Come on. We're going to have to go home and change before we can go anywhere."

"Look at my mega-terrific trousers," Antony said to me. "There's paint all over them."

"Yeah! Look at my super-mega-terrific trousers," Edward said. "I'll never be able to wear them again."

"Your plan was mega useless," Antony said.

"Yeah! Super-duper-mega useless," said Edward.

"But it worked, didn't it?" I said. "After all, we *did* get the spiders off the bench."

We Hate Shopping!

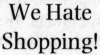

Mum dragged us shopping with her.

We *hate* shopping.

I pushed the trolley whilst Mum read off her list and Antony and Edward got the tins and packets from the shelves.

"Antony, could you get me some plain flour, please?" Mum said, pointing to the right shelf. "The plain flour is in the blue packet."

Antony picked up the packet around its middle.

The top of the packet burst open and WHOOSH! Flour flew up and out – all over Antony's face.

Antony coughed and spluttered and spluttered and coughed. Edward and I cracked up laughing.

It was funny! Antony looked like a ghost.

"I can't take you anywhere," Mum hissed

at Antony as she wiped the white flour off his face.

We carried on walking around the aisles. This time Antony was pushing the trolley and Edward and I were getting the tins and packets.

"Maxine, could you get me some free-range eggs and check them all to make sure they're not cracked?" Mum said.

I picked up the first box of free-range eggs I saw. The trouble was, I picked up the egg box from the top and it wasn't shut properly. The egg box swung open and SPLAT! All the eggs dropped to the floor and right on the foot of the woman standing next to me.

"I'm sorry. It wasn't my fault, the box was already open," I said quickly.

Antony and Edward were holding their stomachs from laughing so hard.

"I'm so sorry," Mum said to the woman with the eggy shoes.

Mum glared down at me. She had her hands on her hips and her eyes were squeezed together and her lips were a thin line.

Boy, was she annoyed!

"It's all right, madam. I'll clean this up,"

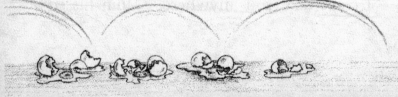

said a man in a chocolate-brown overall. He was holding a bucket and mop.

"I'm sorry about the mess," Mum said, grabbing my hand and pulling me away from the eggy mess on the floor. "Maxine, I can't take you anywhere."

We carried on with our shopping. I *hate* shopping.

This time Mum got Antony and me to push the trolley.

"Edward, could you get me two bottles of lemonade? The ones with the white and green labels over there," Mum said.

Edward picked up two plastic bottles. Mum wandered off to look at the bottles of orange and lemon drink. Edward put one bottle in the trolley but the other one slipped out of his hand and dropped to the floor.

BOING! BOING!

To our surprise, the bottle bounced.

"I didn't know lemonade bottles did that," I said.

Edward picked it up and dropped it to the floor again.

BOING! BOING!

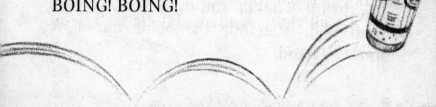

"Edward, what do you think you're doing?"
Mum said, snatching the bottle out of my
brother's hand.

With a frown she turned the bottle cap.

SSSPLOSH! The lemonade flew out everywhere. Over Edward, over Antony, over me – and over the four people standing behind us.

The twins and I laughed until our stomachs hurt and our eyes were watering.

"I ... I was ... er ... just checking the bottle top to make sure it was on properly," Mum stammered. "I'm so sorry. Come on you three. I can't take any of you anywhere!"

Mum dragged us away to where we had to pay.

"I've never been so embarrassed." Mum wagged her finger at all of us. "Edward, you should never shake bottles or cans of fizzy drink because when you open them they explode all over the place."

Mum told us off the entire time we were in the queue waiting to pay for our food. We still thought it was funny until Mum said we couldn't have any sweets for being so naughty. Then Mum made all three of us push the trolley out of the shop.

"It's the only way to keep all of your hands out of trouble," Mum said.

We walked out into the shopping precinct. Mum led the way to the lifts that would take us to the car park. That's where our car was.

Suddenly someone shouted, "Stop those men!"

We looked around and saw a policeman and a policewoman chasing two men – and they were all running in our direction.

"Stop those men!" the policewoman shouted again.

The men were getting closer to us.

Just as they were about to run past us, the twins and I gave our trolley a terrific shove.

The two men ran straight into it. The blond man went flying over our trolley whilst the man with brown hair collapsed on to it.

The policeman and policewoman came running up and then more police arrived from all directions. They grabbed hold of the two men and led them away.

Then two of the police came over to us, bringing our trolley.

"Well done!" the policewoman said to us. "What are your names?"

The twins and I looked at each other.

So I said, "I'm Girl Wonder and . . ."

"We're the Terrific Twins!" said Antony and Edward together.

Hooray!